More praise for John Knoll:

"In an era of downright lies fed on a diet of phoney baloney, John Knoll refreshes and elevates his poetry into prose of heart and soul and place. The Beat breaks through the Hippie facade and the voice of a practical realist tells you stories that, if you heard them read aloud, would make you explode with laughter, then wonder why you laughed. That's true pleasure of John's writing stuck in the American landscape of the Kansas-New Mexico continuum. It's the grit of the sand, the actuality of real people on the page, the insanity of the normal from a truly fully realized American poet/writer. Thank you John Knoll for *Black Mesa Blues!*"

-Larry Goodell, *Nothing to Laugh About*

Other Works by John Knoll:

The Magic Vessel (Be Still Press, 1978)

Wrestling the Wheel (White Buffalo Press, 1982)

Opera of Virus (Long Road Press, 1994)

Elevator Music for the Dead (Long Road/La Cantera Press 2007)

Ghosting America (Lithic Press, 2016)

Hummingbird Graffiti (Beatlick Press, 2019)

Black Mesa Blues

Stories by John Knoll

Kansas City　　Spartan Press　　Missouri

Spartan Press
Kansas City, MO
spartanpresskc.com

Copyright © John Knoll, 2020
First Edition: 1 3 5 7 9 10 8 6 4 2
ISBN: 978-1-952411-31-1
LCCN: 2020946236

Cover art: Jon Lee Grafton
Author's photo: Linda O'Nelio Knoll
All rights reserved. No part of this publication may be
reproduced or transmitted in any form or by any means,
electronic or mechanical, including photocopying,
recording or by info retrieval system, without prior
written permission from the author.

ACKNOWLEDGEMENTS

The poem WALKING CITY STREETS includes lines
from the following poets' poems:

Arthur Rimbaud: The Time of Assassins
Lawrence Ferlinghetti: Populist Manifesto
Vladimir Mayakovski: In the Church of My Heart
Rage Against the Machine: Killing in the Name

I am grateful to the editors who published some of these
poems and stories in their journals and magazines: T*rickster,
High Desert Journal, Lummox Poetry Anthology, BEAT-itude,
Horror Sleaze Trash, Rune Bear* and *Mad Swirl.*

A grant from Moon in the Bucket Fund
helped bring this book to fruition.

Table of Contents:

REMOVEABLE TATTOO / 1

GOING HOME / 7

HOMETOWN BREAKDOWN / 11

A GUY NAMED RON / 17

GRANDMOTHER'S FUNERAL / 19

BLACK HORSE ROCK / 25

KALI ZOO / 29

CROSS-CLEANERS / 32

JOHN HENRY'S ARM / 36

SUNDOWN / 38

THE FIRST TIME I SAW YOUR FACE / 40

THE JADE LOTUS / 42

KILLER AMOEBA / 45

FOURTH OF JULY / 48

COYOTE WOMAN / 56

SNOW FLOWER'S MAY DAY PERFORMANCE / 60

TIME OF ASSASSINS / 61

MARMALADE COCKROACH / 63

JAIL BREAK / 67

PERFORMANCE ART / 71

THE HOLY GHOST BRIGADE / 74

For Jim Hagerman, jazz drummer, warrior,
hands on fire

In memory of Denis Buche, soul mate,
surreal mad man, poet-shaman

*Who put canned laughter
in my crucifixion scene?*

-Charles Simic

REMOVEABLE TATTOO

I hold Frank in my arms. He's dead, shot through the head. We're being overrun. I shake him. I demand that he live. His wide open eyes look right through me. His mother isn't coming. His god isn't coming, just me. Blood flows from his head, connecting the living and the dead. I've never felt this close to anyone. I hear myself praying: Hail Mary! Hail Mary! I piss my pants. The Star Spangled Banner is not playing.

On Friday I was discharged. Saturday I flew out of Bagram Air Base in Afghanistan. Sunday I landed in Albuquerque, from war to civilization in three days. I can't sleep, and when I'm awake, I'm dreaming. I am the war, the hired killer. I had no idea what to do with my life.

I had been home from Afghanistan for three months trying to reconnect with old friends when my friend Gene "the Dream" Macelli offered me a job selling removable tattoos at the New Mexico State Fair in Albuquerque, I accepted, even though the idea seemed crazy, I didn't have anything better to do.

The "Dream" had me dress up like an ink freak. I wore a gold cross around my neck with a red handkerchief tied around my head. The costume highlighted with a red dragon removable tattoo on my left forearm and a Spam tattoo on my neck.

I'm an introvert, but I surprised myself. I got into the role. I started to believe I was a tattooed low-rider from Espanola. I even developed a little carny rap thanks to the script the Dream gave me.

Young women walked down the state fair midway and I yelled out, "Hey pretty mama, come on over here. Let me put a removable tattoo on you; on with water, off with oil. Come on over here and talk to me. I won't hurt you, I promise."

Many of the young ladies would cautiously approach the tattoo booth and ask, "Are they really removable?"

"For sure. For sure. Hey, check out this red rose, and how about this crystal skull. It really looks bad, no? Your boyfriend will love it, especially if you apply it near your heart."

Most women would hesitate for a moment before asking, "Who's going to tattoo my heart?"

"My boss Dr. Macelli is inside the tent here. He's used to seeing all parts of the female anatomy, no problem. Step right in and pay the Doctor. He'll take good care of you and I promise you'll leave the tent with a wonderful tattoo and a sexy new identity."

I couldn't believe how I was acting, but I liked it. It must be the anonymity created by my costume, I thought. It's like wearing a mask and becoming another person.

One night around 10 p.m. a gorgeous dark woman walked towards the tattoo booth with a couple girlfriends. Her blue eyes peered out through a tangle of long black hair. A tattoo of two intertwined snakes around her left bicep. She wore skin tight black jeans and a red Wonder Woman t-shirt.

I tried my best rap on her but she walked on by all proud and sexy. She licked her lips as she walked by me and gave me a faint nod and smile. I waited for her to glance over her shoulder to give me one last look. That didn't happen. She and her two friends turned a corner down by the guy who guessed people's weight and disappeared.

About a half hour later it started to get chilly. "Dream, I'm going to my car to get my jacket," I said. "I'll be right back."

I walked down the carnival's midway with Rolling Stones rock n roll enlivening a night of Ferris wheels and cotton candy. When I got to the parking lot I saw her again. I couldn't believe it. She walked away from me, moving with a dark Latin rhythm.

"Hey, wait up, I want to talk to you."

She stopped and turned.

"I saw you walking past our tattoo booth a little while ago," I said, my throat dry. "How cool that I ran into you again."

"What's your name," she said.

"T.J."

"T.J., why are you following me?"

"I'm not following you. I just stepped off work so I could get a long sleeve shirt for my car."

"And where's your car?"

"You're standing next to it."

"This is sort of funny," she said. "When I passed you I did notice you."

"What's your name," I said.

"Francesca."

She invited me to a party at her house. And there I was at 2 a.m., stumbling down a dark street, trying to find her house. I must have walked up and down the street for over thirty-minutes, dogs barking, lights coming on inside houses. I finally gave up because I was afraid someone might call the police.

I got up around 10 a.m. and went back to find her. This time I found the address. I knocked on the door and an old white haired woman answered.

"Si Senor. Can I help you?"

"Yes. Good morning. I'd like to speak to Francesca."

"How do you know Francesca?"

"I met her last night at the State Fair."

The old woman looked at him with a deep sadness in her eyes.

"Senor, my daughter Francesca died at birth."

I was stunned.

"What do you mean? There must be a mistake. I saw Francesca last night."

"I'm sorry. Many men have had this vision. Many men have held my daughter in the night." And she closed the door.

I was overwhelmed, close to tears. The world started to spin as I walked away. Then I heard what sounded like Francesca's voice.

"Come back, T.J. I was just playing with you."

I turned and saw the old woman in the doorway. She pulled off her wig.

"T.J., I was trying on my make-up and costume for the Lorca play I'm in. I'm sorry. I didn't mean to frighten you. It just happened spontaneously. Come on in the house."

I walked past her and entered the house. Before I could say a word she kissed me, took my hand and lead me into the bedroom, we fell into bed, tearing at each other's clothes. For the first time in my life, I made love to a woman.

After we made love I didn't know why, but I was disappointed. I could see Francesca was disappointed too. It wasn't what I had expected. I rolled out of bed and put on my clothes.

"I have to go to work," I said.

"Will you come by tonight?"

"For sure,"

The next night, after drinking a couple of beers, we started to make love again.

"You know T.J., it was nice making love to you last night, but you didn't have your penis inside me. It was between my thighs."

I never felt so embarrassed.

Francesca had to stifle a giggle and I gave out a nervous laugh. We made love for the first time, again. She was an experienced, skillful lover, making love to a virgin. I followed her instructions.

"Fuck me harder, T.J. Harder. I want you to hurt me. Choke me until I come."

I went too far.

GOING HOME

Dwayne Evans feels like he has just escaped prison. He drives out of Los Angeles after living in Venice Beach for three years where the shit meets the sea. He listens to Noise, a band he formed and deformed. Then bam, his car throws a rod and there's the bing, bang, screech boom, metal against metal. Hell on I-40 about twenty miles west of Flagstaff.

"Fuck it," he mantras out loud. I can't believe it. He thinks about all the stories his dad told him about hitch-hiking in the 60s and 70s. Why not, I know people say you can't hitchhike safely in the 21st Century. What choice do I have?

He stands on the shoulder of I-40. Thumb in the air, committing the misdemeanor of hitch-hiking on an interstate. Trucking east to New Mexico, a tricked out Camaro speeds by, ignores his thumb. Tires screech, he turns around.

The Camaro pulls over about 100 yards down the interstate. He picks up his duffle bag and runs towards the car. He gets about 10 feet from the car and it takes off, spitting gravel in his face.

"Mother-fucker," he yells, and gives him the finger.

The car goes a short distance and pulls over again. This time he walks to the car. The passenger door flies open and he hears a laughing voice, "Get in this car white boy. We've got a long journey ahead of us."

He looks into the car and sees a guy with long black hair. Good vibe. He throws his duffle bag in the back seat.

"My name's Dante," he says.

"Dwayne Evans. Thanks for stopping."

"What are you doing hitch-hiking? I haven't seen a hitch-hiker since I left L.A."

"My car threw a rod. I just left it. It's not worth fixing."

"Where are you going?"

"Taos. To see my mom and dad."

"Hey, no kidding. I'm on my way to my grandmother's funeral in Taos, but after that I plan to go to Santa Fe. I got a job offer down there."

"Nice."

"Hey, I hate to ask, but do you have any money?"

"I can help you out."

"Thanks man. I don't know how I'm going to make it to Taos. But I'll get there. I have to. My Grandmother just died and I have to get to her funeral."

Dante drives into the night. They drink a couple beers and smoke weed listening to rock n roll radio.

"My grandfather's name was Riding Two Horses," Dante says. "He was a Sioux chief. Grandfather could ride two horses at the same time. He would stand bare foot on their bare backs and ride like the wind. I saw him do it many times."

Dante glances at the gas gauge, breaking off his story. "We're almost out of gas. Damn, I guess I'll have to sell my spare tire."

"Come on. Don't sell your tire. I've got a few dollars."

"I'm just kidding."

Dwayne thinks about the car load of Chicanos that picked him up outside Las Vegas, New Mexico. There wasn't room in the car or the car trunk for his duffle bag so they threw their spare tire in the ditch to make room for him. He could still see the tire rolling down the hill in the dusky New Mexico summer light.

They were drunk, smoking weed and drinking Coors. A guy offered him a beer and he said, "No thanks, I'm boycotting Coors."

"What's wrong esse?" a guy name Felipe said. "Are you prejudiced against Coors or something?"

Weird how memories pop up out of nowhere.

"All right, we're gassed up," Dante says. "Let's stop up here at McDonald's and buy a couple cheeseburgers. I haven't eaten all day."

They roll on, "more or less in time", feasting on Big Macs, with Dante telling stories.

"I graduated from South Dakota State two years ago with a Journalism degree," Dante says between bites. "So, I'm in South Dakota with a Journalism B.A. but there are no journalism jobs, especially if you're Native. I left the Rez and went out to Los Angeles. I stayed with my aunt for three months before I finally got a job working for a weekly newpaper. I worked there six months before they laid me off. So here I am now, just like you, going back to visit our memories."

They burn another one and Dwayne falls asleep. Dante cranks up the Rolling Stones, pushes on towards his Grandmother's funeral.

Dwayne wakes and notices it's 8 a.m. on the car's clock. They come up over a rise and he sees the Taos Gorge for the first time in three years. He's home.

"Thanks for the ride, brother. I hope we connect again."

"You never know," Dante says.

HOMETOWN BREAKDOWN

Dwayne catches a cab to his parent's home on Salazar Street. He has the cab driver drive around town but his hometown isn't there anymore; the three-story red bricked high school torn down, the Last Resort Pool Hall gone, Denton's Funeral Home now a bank.

Late afternoon sunlight diffuse and muted like underwater light flickers through a line of darkening catalpa trees. The cab pulls into his parent's driveway. He notices his Dad's silver Cadillac parked in the garage.

He's ambivalent about seeing his parents but they were getting old and he felt it his duty to visit them more often. For two years he made excuses on the telephone about why he couldn't come home for Thanksgiving or Christmas. He feels guilty.

Dwayne pays the cabby and tips him five dollars. "Thanks Dwayne," the cabby says. "Good to see you again."

"Yeh, Bobby Joe, good to see you too."

Dwayne and Bobby Joe played football together on their undefeated football team. Bobby Joe would go home that night and tell his wife Brenda, "Dwayne Evans is back in town. I picked him up at the bus station today."

"Really, I wonder what he's doing back in town? Last I heard he was living in L.A."

"That boy never gives up. He's what 34 years old and he's still trying to become an actor."

Dwayne pulls his orange sport's bag from the cab's back seat, walks down the driveway past the red bricked chimney where his brother Gary hid his candy in the ash box. The white stone swan still on the back lawn next to the flagpole. He walks in the back door without knocking as was his custom when he came home in the past. When his mother sees him she stops talking on the telephone and her face flushes because he caught her off guard. Betsy, her toy poodle, barks at him and nips at his ankles. He gives the dog a playful kick.

"Betsy, you stop it now. Don't you remember Dwayne? Doris, I'll call you back. Dwayne's home."

Oprah on the nine inch back and white kitchen television, talks about the growing opioid addiction among rural teenagers. Dwayne puts his bag down, glares at the neurotic ankle biting dog and walks towards his mother to give her a kiss. She doesn't let him kiss her, rather she turns her head and they give each other a brief hug.

"How are you doing Mom?"

"Pretty good. I'm a little tired. How are you?"

"A little tired," he says.

"How long did it take you to get here?"

"About 18 hours."

"Are you hungry?" she asks, opening the refrigerator.

Before he can answer his dad walks into the kitchen dressed in his pajamas.

"Dad," his dad says, "I didn't know you were here. I thought you were working today."

"This isn't your dad, God-damn it," Maxine says. "This is your son, Dwayne."

"Always bullshitting me, aren't you Maxine. Do you think I'm nuts, or what? I know who this is."

Dwayne grabs his dad and gives him a big hug.

"Don't do that Father White," his dad says. "You know I don't like being hugged by a priest, especially priests like you who park their elephants in my garage."

"Dad," Dwayne says, "it's me Dwayne. I've come home to visit for a few days."

"Look out the window, look at the Black Raiders riding white horses through our back yard. That's just not right. What did you say your name is? I've got to get to work but first of all I need to find my baseball glove. Maxine is my mother coming over to put up the Christmas tree?"

"Your mother's been dead for two years, Paul."

"Now I know that's not true."

His dad turns away and limps back into his bedroom to watch a football game on TV. "Mom," Dwayne says, "why didn't you tell me dad is in such bad condition?"

"How in the hell could I tell you? I haven't heard from you for four years."

"It hasn't been that long."

"Whatever."

He slumps into a chair. The room spins. He stares pure hate into the little rat dog that bites everyone that enters the house. "If I ever spend time with this dog, I'm going to kill it," he almost murmurs out loud.

"I had no idea his Alzheimer's was this bad," he says. He runs his fingers through his oily black hair, lowering his eyes in shame. He feels demons in the room, looks out the bay window into the backyard where an American flag hangs limp on the silver flag pole.

"Well, I can't take care of the poor bastard anymore," Maxine says. She takes a long drag on her cigarette, blows a smoke ring. "I'm putting him in a rest home."

Dwayne stands up, rage makes him tremble. He walks to the Mr. Coffee, pulls a red mug from the cabinet and pours a cup of two hour old coffee.

"Would you like some cobbler?"

"What? You have cobbler? No, I don't want any."

Maxine's jaw drops. "What, you love blackberry cobbler."

"I used to." He moves closer to her. Invades her space. "Look mom, I'm going to move back and take care of dad. I..."

Maxine slams the hot cobbler on the kitchen counter top, says, "Don't make me laugh. You can't even take care of yourself and you're almost 40 years old."

"I don't want dad in a rest home. I'm..."

"You're not going to do shit Dwayne Evans. I love the old bastard and I'm doing what's best for everybody. It's my only choice."

"It's not your only choice. Just listen to me for once in your life." He feels himself losing self-control. Regains a temporary balance by focusing on his breath, a disciple he developed in war, two failed marriages and a year in Leavenworth.

"I'm moving back," he says. "I'll take care of Dad." He sobs into his hands covering his face. sees his first wife and her boyfriend making love in his Cadillac, sees blood run from the stomach of a pregnant women he shot because she was about to blow up the mosque where the CIA ran "Operation Mirror."

"Dwayne Evans you're pitiful. You know that. You're goddamn pathetic. Why don't you go and take care of yourself? And if you're going to come around here causing trouble like you always do you might as well leave right now. You've lost your soul ever since you started dating whores. Your first wife, Valarie, was making love to half the people in town. What a slut, and your second wife, that insane Mary Ellen, what a piece of work she was. You're a loser and you fall in love with losers."

Mother dear, you are the Ice Queen a narcissistic bitch. He knows if he stays with her any longer he would lose control. His legs feel numb. His mouth dry. He walks to the back door, picks up his duffle bag and turns towards his mother.

Maxine turns her back on him. She wipes the stove top with a dishrag. Oprah just signing off. He looks around the room one last time, sees his high school graduation picture, a crucifix on the knotty pine wall and a framed picture of Jesus, the one where his eyes follow you wherever you go.

He wants to say, "Mom, can't we talk?" as he leaves the house, but he knows they can't.

A GUY NAMED RON

Dante finds himself sitting at a bar stool next to a Texan. A guy named Ron. Dante knows the guy's name is Ron because R-O-N is etched on his big silver Texas belt buckle.

Ron likes to talk. Dante pretends to listen. "I lost a couple pounds of cocaine and these three beaners were kicking the shit out of me because they fronted me and they were passionate about wanting their coke. I tried to explain my position that I was ripped off in Tijuana, but they didn't believe my story, so I pulled my .38 from my boot just to get their attention."

He continues his story, Dante drinks a beer, listens to Ron rant about blood, neon lit skull bones flying through the motel window, screams and the smell of fear.

After he killed off the guys in his story his adrenalin begins to subside and he says, "After that deal gone bad I decided to change careers. I went back to school and got a B.S in Computer Science. You see, Dante, I want to teach at the university level. When I walk across a campus in the early morning sunlight it almost makes me believe in god."

"You must really love teaching Computer Science," Dante says.

"No son, you don't understand. It's the soft feminine light that turns me on." Ron says, plunging a toothpick into his drunken grin.

Ron orders beer for the house. He and Dante are the only customers in the bar. He takes off on another story. "I have a friend coaching high school basketball in New Mexico. I wish I was a coach. I used to coach little league baseball. If you want I'll tell you my coaching philosophy.

"Feed the kids lots of chocolate. Brain wash them into believing they're direct descendants of the Iowa Corn God, get them new Nikes, drink lots of water and get lots of rest. And ideally, they shouldn't masturbate on game day. I learned that from my high school football coach. That's about the extent of my coaching philosophy, Dante. O yeh, one more thing. Learn voodoo and hex your opponents with a chicken foot, the evil eye, a crucifix or whatever it takes. That's what Notre Dame does. Am I lying? What works works, Dante, am I lying? You tell me. I'm woke, son. I'm woke."

Ron rests his head on the bar and passes out.

GRANDMOTHER'S FUNERAL

I

Before my Grandmother's funeral, I felt like visiting the house where she lived for sixty years. I find the key where it's always been, under a red brick next to the back steps. As I step inside I smell Grandmother's perfume. The sweet smell of death lingers. Night crawls in the kitchen window. I contemplate a framed picture of Jesus on the kitchen wall above the table where my coal-digging Grandfather often sat and drank coffee, muscles bulging through a white wife-beater undershirt. Jesus opens and closes his eyes when I walk by his picture. And now Grandfather walks in the door. He carries a gunnysack filled with fish: blue-gill, bass, crappie, and a bull-head catfish. In the window behind him, lightning flashes. I count: one, two, three, four and thunder rumbles Grandmother's china. Grandmother cooks on a wood-burning stove. She sweats scorpions, cooks frog legs that twitch around the cast-iron skillet doing a sizzling death dance that turns Grandfather on. Grandfather walks to the center of the kitchen, empties the gunny-sack on the black and white checkered linoleum floor and fish flop like birds trying to fly. His white muscle shirt drips black coal blood. Jesus opens and closes his eyes. I bend to pick up a fish. "Don't you touch that fish," Grandmother says. I don't but don't understand why. I count the wrinkles on Grandmother's face. One by one the fish begin to disappear. When catfish disappear there's a popping sound. When a bass goes it's a violin string being tuned. One by one all fish dematerialize. The framed picture of Jesus disappears. Lightning flashes outside the window and illuminates Grandmother's face and the black island of her eyes. Then pop, Grandfather is no longer here. Another flash of lightning slithers across the kitchen floor like a white snake. A hand reaches out and touches my cheek "Listen, Dante. Listen," Grandmother says. A dark haunting melody screws itself up from the kitchen drain. Lightning illuminates a halo of butterflies around Grandmother's head. Then zap zap, Grandmother disappears, the white snake too. Out the window, I see a lilac bush burst into flame. Thunder rattles the windows.

II

I sit in an adobe church two blocks from the Taos Plaza, attending Grandmother's funeral, her ashes in a blue vase between an American flag and a picture of Jesus petting a lamb whose neck is slit. I look out a window, lightning flickers, flashes and strobes the congregation. I'm wrong, it's not lightning. It's a herd of huge golden butterflies on wing strobing the morning light with telepathic florescent wings. In the church, no one seems to notice. A right-wing-Nazi-born-again ex-football playing Christian minister holds up a black book with B-I-B-L-E inscribed on the cover. He quotes the Book of John, the Book of Matthew, The Book of Amos, and the Book of Andy. He says the black book says that Jesus is the one and only way into heaven. Outside the mutant butterflies begin to brush against the white church walls, creating a vibration, causing the huge crucifix next to the American flag to fall off the wall. The born again preacher keeps on preaching, says, "Thank God I'm a Christian because only Christians can be saved." On impulse, without thinking, I stand up and shout, "Metaphor. Metaphor." The preacher shouts back, "You, sir, are the anti-Christ." I'm about to retort but the golden butterflies are at the windows, butting their coal-black heads in a furious John Coltrane spiritual rhythm. I begin to chant, "A Love Supreme. A Love Supreme. A Love Supreme." The butterflies crash through the windows, swoop in and carry the preacher, the crucifix, the flag and the slaughtered lamb out the front door. A sudden silence like before a tornado follows their exit. No one speaks. The congregation sits in silence until nightfall, and then they file out single file into the night. I walk towards my pickup, chant: "A Love Supreme. A Love Supreme." A tiny flame flickers above the blue vase in the hands of my Grandfather as he walks towards the plaza and disappears into a snow storm.

III

The night after Grandmother's funeral, I left the rez and drove into Taos. I wanted to have a couple beers in my old hangout, The Last Resort. I took a seat at the bar. Mick Jagger and the Stones blossomed from speakers above the bar's back mirror: "You might not get what you want, but if you try sometime you just might find you get what you need." I thought, that's bullshit. The truth is you never get want you need but you might sometimes get what you want. I watched a couple cowboys arm wrestle in the mirror while I drank my beer.

I arm wrestled a lot when I was in college. College was way gone but I felt the need to throw down with the young Anglo cowboys. A muscular red headed kid won the match; he turned on his chair and issued a loud challenge. "Anybody want a part of me?"

"Let's see what you've got my friend," I said.

The kid looked at me, laughed and said, "The old redskin is feeling his oats."

I sat at the table across from the kid. "Kid," I said, placing my foot against a wooden rail beneath the table for extra leverage, "I haven't arm wrestled for seventeen years."

The kid gazed bad into my eyes. "You about ready to go, Chief?"

We locked hands. Someone said, "Go."

Rap music bounced off the walls of the Last Resort. Neither hand moved an inch. I began to fade. The Kid pulled my hand towards the table. Then magic happened. The spirits of the dead entered me, the killing fields, the weeping women and children at Sand Creek, Wounded Knee, Bear River, and the Trail of Tears. I felt the crazy wisdom soul of Geronimo, Crazy Horse, Cochise, and Peltier. I felt buffalo in my blood, rumbling like thunder. I felt the strength of my dead Grandfather going down into the underground coal mines. Dark and criminal my eye's glazed over; I went into a trance, spirit power resurrected like an old god being reborn.

Hooked hand in hand with a red-neck cowboy, all that existed was the awareness of a breathing beast fighting for his life. I had the feeling I couldn't lose, that feeling, that indescribable feeling, my Grandfather used to say of knowing where the balls going before it's hit, knowing where the halfback will be before the halfback knows. I pulled the kid's arm through Afghanistan, down into Vietnam, the killing fields of the Arizona desert, through drunken nights with women whose names I can't remember.

Come on Kid, come on down with me to El Chapultepec Bar downtown Denver. Come listen to Lou Reed with me. Come on down and sleep in the alley with me. I pulled the Kid through Mexico City avenues past the bloated bellies of starving children. Let's go Kid, you're going down with me down to the roots of rain, to the place where the dead talk. I'm taking you down Kid. I'm taking you home. I pulled the Kid's hand to the table top, gently like a feather floating to the desert floor, kissing the hot sand. There was a moment of silence.

"Goddamn, you're good old man," the Kid said. "You Indians are stronger than you look."

"And you're as stupid as you look, son."

The kid's friends didn't have to hold him back. I chugged a beer and left the bar.

BLACK HORSE ROCK

Dante, Dwayne and I had been partying for several hours in the Rio Grande bosque west of Otowi Bridge, when Dwayne said, "Let's climb Black Mesa."

"Are you drunk?" Dante asked.

"I'm bored."

"That's sacred land you know."

"All land is sacred."

"I guess if we climb the mesa and pray while we climb we'll be alright," Dante said.

"That's a weak excuse, bro. But I'll buy it." I said.

We jumped in Dwayne's truck and began a zigzag journey up and down across arroyos and into the juniper hills surrounding Black Mesa. Golden cottonwood trees lined the banks of the Rio Grande. Warren Zevon on the radio sang a blues song about Indian Casino Bingo.

"Dwayne, you're scaring the hell out of me with your cowboy driving," I said.

"Puss," he said, and let out a loud howl.

I worried the Pueblo Police might see the truck and we would spend a few nights in an Indian jail.

Dwayne drove his truck as far as he could without tipping over on the steep slope and parked it behind a clump of juniper trees.

We got down and found a volcanic rock trail to the top of the mesa. I stumbled a couple of times and wished I had remembered to bring my walking stick. Dwayne, with Dionysian glee, jumped from black rock to black rock like a wacked out halfback. .

It took about forty five minutes to climb to the top. The view was like a postcard you send to your friends in the city. The Rio Grande slid by and disappeared into the canyons at the foot of Los Alamos. To the east the Sangre de Cristos imitated their name. Late afternoon sunlight poured in over the snow-capped Jemez Mountains to the west.

Black Mesa had a haunted feel like stepping into another time when humans could understand the language of bees. Medicine Wheels, birthing stones, pot shards, human skulls, thigh bones, horse bones and raven feathers.

We realized we were on holy ground but our sense of right and wrong was exceeded by our zeal to explore the mysteries of Black Mesa.

It didn't take much of an imagination to hear tribal drums, to see dancers dressed like deer and elk.

"We shouldn't be here," Dante said

"Let's get out of here guys," I said. "We have to go before the Indian police see us."

"We should leave this place," Dante said, picking up on the same vibes I felt. "This place is on Holy Ground."

"Ah, come on Dante, we just got here," Dwayne said. "Let's look around."

Dwayne, a new age shaman, sat atop a huge penis shaped rock next to a womb rock and said, "I hear songs of the old gods." I started down the trail without commenting on Dwayne's hubris, Dante followed. Halfway down, Dwayne caught up. We walked in silence.

On the way back to my house, Dwayne pulled a rock from his shirt pocket. "Check this out, T.J." He showed me a black rock engraved with a horse.

"You have to take it back."

"No, I can't. It spoke to me."

"I don't want anything to do with your stealing holy objects," Dante said. "Return the damn rock."

"It's not stealing. It's magic. Black horse rocks are magic."

Dwayne refused to return the stone. "This is fate," he said. "This was meant to be."

The next day, Dwayne drove his truck west into the glare of a setting sun. He came up over a hill and had a head on collision with a black horse that was running down the middle of the highway. The horse slid over the hood into the windshield and continued to slide into the pickup's bed. Dwayne was blinded by the glass, lost control and rolled the truck into an arroyo. Bad Karma. I worried he's wife might have a miscarriage. Thank god she gave birth to a healthy boy.

KALI ZOO

Francesca stands naked at a living room window and stares into the night, listening to a coyote choir. She begins to bark and howl; a howl that sounds close to a scream. Her body is outlined by the moon, illuminating her firm, athletic body. She moves to an unheard rhythm with a sensuous grace. She dances into trance and chants: "I am giving birth to the black waters of time. My hands are Aztec flowers reaching deep into my heritage. I am Kali, chewing cocks, spitting blood, hair and teeth. My.....

"Francesca, what the hell are you doing?" I yell from my office.

"What?"

"What are you doing?"

"You've interrupted me again."

"O sorry, I interrupted you barking at a window"

I walk into the room. There is a moment of silence, like the silence before a tornado. We stare ferocious red light into one another's eyes that magnifies the demons of our failing relationship.

"So you stand at the window, howling at the moon and I'm…."

"I wasn't howling at the moon. I was howling at the coyotes to be quiet"

The room is illuminated with over two dozen candles, shadows flicker on the wall.

"And I heard you saying something about you are Kali, chewing cocks…."

"I'm rehearsing for my performance at La Cucaracha. Now, please leave me alone."

"You know, your performance art is such bull-shit."

"You're right. It's such bull-shit that I'm moving to New York because doing performance art in New Mexico is like doing Shakespeare on a used car lot in the middle of the desert."

"Shakespeare on a used car lot in the middle of the desert?" You're always on aren't you? Always playing to the crowd even when you're alone. I'm going out. Later."

I leave the house and five minutes later Anita Franklin knocks on the Francesca's door. "Come in, Anita," Francesca screams. "Come in."

Anita throws her coat on the sofa and says, "You're in a good mood."

"O fuck you, Anita."

'You guys are fighting again?"

"Duh."

"Do you have any wine?"

"Help yourself."

"Let's go dancing. You want to?"

"You know, I kind of do, but first I have to finish rehearsing. You can be the audience."

"Do I have to? Just kidding. But I have a sense you're about ready to get weird on me."

"Just listen, Anita. Listen. Primitive dreams. A sax. I dance naked in moonlight."

"Have you been taking your medication?"

Francesca ignores her. She dances to her poem: "I am giving birth to the black water of time. My hands are paddles reaching deep into my heritage. I am Kali, chewing cocks, spitting blood, hair and teeth. My body tri-angulated against the yellow moon. I am giving birth. My womb empty. I am dying flying beyond the sound of time. I am golden corn wolf crow stone. I grow wings and marry three white horses. I multiply myself. The oceans fold around my breast. I am drowning. I yearn to lie beneath the Sangre de Cristos. My breath of seaweed. My touch of pine. My smile Satanic. I am Goddess. I am Old. I am Virgin. I am Whore. I am. I am. Kali."

The poem ends. Francesca blows out the candles.

"I'm worried about you Francesca. Are you getting into Black Magic?"

"Anita, sometimes you are insufferable. Speaking of magic, Zoo is performing Homoerotic Assassination tonight."

"Let me guess. I bet Jaime's in the play."

"I bet your right."

"I thought you were going to give him up."

"I can't. I don't even want to."

"If T.J. finds out…"

"He's not going to find out. He's so naïve. I got home at three last week and told him I ran out of gas. If he suspects anything, I just give him a blow job and he's all lovey-dovey."

"You're a bad girl. A bad, bad girl. I'd like to go with you but I have to pick up the kids from the baby sitter."

CROSS-CLEANERS

T.J.

What do you hate the most?

Francesca:
(thinking)

T.J.

Shopping at Wal-Mart? Driving rush hour traffic? Government bureaucracy?

Francesca

Just shut up. Will you please shut up? I hate your patriarchal prompting. Like I can't even think of what I hate without you prompting me.

T.J.

So that's what you hate the most?

Francesca

What?

T.J.:

You hate me because I'm a man.

Francesca

I didn't say that.

T.J.

Then what did you mean when you said you hate my patriarchal prompting?

Francesca

You're so screwed up. You know that?

T.J.

You hate patriarchy more than anything. Admit it.

Francesca

No, I hate housekeeping more than anything. I hate housework more than I hate you. I could easily leave you, never see your sad ass face again, but housework is always there. Wherever I go, there it is, dirt; dog shit on the rug, cat piss on the sofa, dirty dishes. I hate it. Housecleaning never goes away. Never will. Never. Never. Never.

T.J.:

I'm sorry you feel that way.

Francesca

You're what? Don't you patronize me, you son-of-a-bitch.

T.J.

There you go with that feminist rap again. I'm not
patronizing you. I'm just disagreeing with you
because housecleaning is like sex for me.
It's getting your hands in forbidden places,
like cleaning shit out of the toilet bowl
and secretly taking off your rubber gloves.

Francesca

You're sick.

T.J.

O come on now. You know I'm a liar.
And I'd appreciate it
if you would quit interrupting me.

Francesca

I'm not interrupting you.

T.J.

Yes, you are.

Francesca

O excuse me. Please go on. It's just that I'm so literal. I didn't
realize you were
speaking metaphorically.

T.J.

Thank-you. You see housecleaning is like sex because it has to be done and when I'm finished I feel so much better, so clean, so pure. If fact, in a lot of ways house cleaning is better than sex.

Francesca

Then why don't you do more housecleaning if it's so god-damn sexy?

T.J.

Because I'm repressed.

JOHN HENRY'S ARM

Miles Davis played Kind of Blue, I stood next to an abstract expressionist painting, a cacophonous riot of black, red and gold and executed a James Brown spin.

Thirteen candles scattered around the room flickering shadows on adobe walls. Above an adobe fireplace, a winged-serpent hovered over a burning manuscript, black ash like tiny birds fluttered around the room.

Pointing to the upper left hand corner of the painting, I said, "Francesca, can you see John Henry's arm in the painting?"

"I see a canvas of abstract colors," she said. "How you see John Henry's arm I'll never know. Sometimes I think you're crazy."

"Francesca, sometimes I think I'm crazy."

I took a drink of Japanese beer, danced around the room with drunken biker grace.

"I'm a butterfly," I said, "a dying butterfly."

I chanted my favorite mantra: A-E-I-O-U, danced until I passed out.

A soft knock at the front door.

I open the door. It's Toshi, my dream lover, she's barefoot, a Little Red Riding Hood picnic basket over her left forearm, filled with red roses, dead fish and a rabbit's head.

"Is this a good time to visit?"

Behind her, through a sand storm, I see a rain slicked palm tree made of human skin. The sky of orange whispers above the streets of Kabul. Toshi wears a yellow mini-skirt and a Mickey Mouse t-shirt. Her long black hair reminds me of Blue, my childhood pet butterfly.

I hear a crashing sound behind my back, turn towards the sound, nothing there. When I turn back towards Toshi she's disappeared. Rose petals swirl in the wind like undelivered kisses.

Curled up like a sigil in a renaissance alchemical text my morning consciousness came slowly with arthritic pain, alcohol pain, bad marriage pain, Catholic pain, the pain of war, red rose pain, back pain and the disappearance of Toshi, my angel of light.

SUNDOWN

Dante sits on his back porch, his purple heart pinned to a blue work shirt. He kills a can of beer, shoots grasshoppers off the weeds with his .22. The darker it got the better he shot. "We just can't let nature take its course anymore," he says, "everyone needs a flame thrower."

THE FIRST TIME I SAW YOUR FACE

I'm stalled in an I-25 rush hour traffic jam. Five days a week for the last six months, I've endured traffic jams on my ninety minute commute from my job as a body guard in Albuquerque to my home in Santa Fe. I'd like to shoot myself in the face.

I pull a miniature vodka from under the front seat, pour it into a plastic water bottle and take a drink. I've learned to pace my drinking; one miniature on the way to work, one at lunch and one more on my way home.

Finally home, I pull in the driveway, anxious to take off this monkey suit and take a shower. I rip off my tie, walk into the house and hear Roberta Flack singing "The First Time I Ever Saw Your Face" blaring from the radio.

"Francesca, are you home?"

No answer.

I climb the stairs and find her in the bedroom folding clothes. She says hello without missing a beat in her clothes folding ritual. I try to kiss her, she turns away.

"We have to talk," she says.

I plop down on the bed. Flack's lyrics fill the house: "The first time I ever saw your face, the sun and the moon...." Francesca, still folding clothes, says, "I want a divorce."

I knew she was having an affair. How could I not know? Her habitual half-assed excuses about why she got home at 4 a.m., things like I had a flat tire, my friend Sharon was depressed and suicidal, a man took me to the mountains and I had to talk him out of raping me. All this and she would come home smelling of sex.

Still I'm stunned by the abruptness of her statement and all I can say is, "Why?"

She drops the towel she's folding, says, "I don't love you."

"Are you in love with someone else?" I ask sarcastically

"It doesn't matter why," she says. "I want a divorce."

Volcanic rage swells up in my body. A feral grin creases my face. I want to kill her. In my imagination a bloody knife appears in my hand and she lies dead in a pool of blood.

I dance around her body, knife in hand and sing: "I've got a fish love for you Francesca because I like the way you taste." My song becomes a series of wailing screeches like a hyena in labor. The wailing subsides. I chant, "I'm going to bring you back to life just like Jesus being resurrected. I'm going cut you up and eat you. You'll become one with me…"

If I had a therapist they would love this fantasy, I thought as I drive away, early evening shadows slide up the blood red Sangre de Cristo Mountains.

THE JADE LOTUS

Two a.m., I finished my tequila and sketched out the plot of a story called The Jade Lotus. The Jade Lotus is a massage parlor in Paris. Kristina, a young masseuse from Romania, falls hopelessly in love with Victor, an American professor who winds up in her massage parlor by accident, dragged there by his buddies after a fateful evening of booze and drugs. Victor pays for an hour of sex, but he doesn't touch her. He asks her to remove her clothes and lie on the bed while he tells her his sexual fantasies. They see each other several more times, whenever she isn't working, but Victor must leave to finish his teaching duties at a small college in England.

In Paris, Kristina waits expectantly while continuing to satisfy the needs of her numerous clients. Though pure at heart, she fervently jerks off and sucks paunchy, mustached Italians and corpulent, bald Americans. Finally, during summer break Victor returns and tries to free her from her hell - but the Romanian mafia doesn't see things in quite the same light. Victor persuades the American ambassador and the president of a humanitarian organization opposed to the exploitation of young girls to intervene and he's able to free her.

The night before their marriage, Kristina gives, for the first time, an honest account of the extent of her sexual experience. Victor wasn't surprised. In fact it fired his desire for her.

"Our genitals are a source of impermanent, accessible pleasure," Kristina said. "The god who created our misfortune, who made us short-lived, vain and cruel, has also provided this form of meagre compensation."

How could he disagree, but a common problem at the beginning of Victor's three marriages is that despite the initial sexual urgency he experiences an unpleasant sense of having reached an end in a ready built monogamous structure. This he knew was a common feeling, the loss of individuality, the end in the beginning.

He has completely lost the sense of giving. Try as he might, he no longer feels sex as something natural. Not only does he grow bored with her body, but he no longer feels truly attracted to her body. It's impossible to make love without a certain abandon. At 54, Victor has become cold, rational and acutely conscious of his individual existence. On top of that he's obsessed with health and hygiene, hardly ideal conditions for love.

With the Coronavirus pandemic, Victor and Kristina have been isolated in their one bedroom apartment for six months. Their arguments have become more frequent and violent. Tonight at a supper of stuffed chicken breasts, brown rice and broccoli, Kristina broke the heavy silence and said, "I'm not going to talk for the rest of the month." Victor laughed a sarcastic laugh and said, "I'll believe it when I see it. You have the discipline of a three year old." She threw her glass of wine at him. "You're an ass-hole," she said and stormed out of the room.

Three a.m., he sits alone in the living room, watching TV with the sound turned off, only the sound of traffic on the street below. Kristina's in bed, unable to sleep, making plans for her escape to Bucharest, her home town, where she hopes to enroll in the university and study law. Victor gets up and walks to a wall safe. He opens the safe, pulls out a Beretta M9, pours himself a tequila and sits back down in front of the TV. Tenderly, he strokes the pistol lying on his lap.

KILLER AMOEBA

I crouched behind the red rocks above Spence Springs in the Jemez Mountains and waited, transfixed by the turquoise blue sky. I thought about the first time Francesca and I went to Spence Springs. Was it 2018, 2019? It didn't matter.

I don't remember the year, but the month, I remember was May. I remember the Beatles, singing: "Here comes the sun…" The rising sun nestled in the mountain peaks like the golden eye of God.

Looking down into the Spence Springs parking lot I saw a red Porsche drive up. Francesca and her boyfriend stepped out of the car. I watched them disappear and reappear on the winding trail that led up to the hot springs. She seemed to hesitate a moment when she came to the river crossing, something she wouldn't have done in the past.

The river crossing was precarious. There was snow and ice on the pine log lying across the river. He walked across first to show her that it could be done. She followed, tentatively.

They climbed a well-marked trail towards the steaming springs. When they get to the springs, they stood and talked for a moment. I wished I could hear their conversation. After a few minutes they undressed and stepped naked into the healing waters. I thought I could hear her sigh.

Shortly after getting in the water, they smoked a joint. Some things never change. Soon they were making love. Their bodies shrouded by steam, like ghosts.

After they left the springs and walked back towards the parking lot I climbed down to the springs and dipped a small bottle into the water. I twisted a red cap on the bottle and sang, "Yesterday life was such an easy game to play…"

That night, back in my Santa Fe apartment, I phoned her and invited her and her boyfriend over for a sample of my most recent acquisition, seven grams of pure Colombian cocaine. I could feel her nose twitch as she immediately said, "Sure, we'll be over in about an hour. Would you like us to bring anything?"

"No," I said. "I've got everything we need."

We did one line, two; listened to the latest Neville Brothers tape, smoked a doobie, drank red wine and did another line.

"My nose is dry," I said. "How about you guys? Want to moisten up?"

I went to the refrigerator, twisted a red cap off a bottle, and poured the spring water into a blue glass.

She poured a little water into her palm and sniffed a few drops of water. Her boyfriend did the same. "Ah," she sighed, "that's better, much better."

Before Francesca and her boyfriend left Spence Springs they glanced at a Forest Service sign written in Spanish: "Aviso. No inhalas la aqua…" They didn't speak or read Spanish. If they could they would have read: "Warning. Do not inhale the water through your nose. The water contains micro-organisms that when inhaled can be harmful to your health."

The previous week's edition of the Santa Fe Reporter had an article about the waters of Spence Springs. It said the waters contained amoeba that when inhaled travel to the brain and immediately begin to ingest the brain's proteins. Death usually occurs within 2-4 hours after ingestion.

As they left my apartment they both complained of slight headaches. I gave them two Tylenol and told them to drive carefully.

FOURTH OF JULY

Dwayne and Bernadette Silva turned off New Mexico's Highway 502 about a mile after crossing the Rio Grande on Otowi Bridge. Their Mercury's headlights illuminated a little wooden cross stuck in the ground beside a cholla cactus. A couple days earlier Erik, the party's host, told Dwayne he stuck the cross there to keep human coyotes away.

Dwayne drove into the bosque, mostly tall cottonwoods, a few juniper and pinyon. The river could be heard echoing off canyon walls. A huge bonfire was visible through the trees. They were late arrivals to the party and the road was lined with cars and pickups, mostly pickups. He parked in a spot next to a sweat lodge.

Before getting out of the car, he reached in the back sit and opened a cooler filled with ice and pulled out a beer. He opened one for Bernadette and they walked towards the bonfire, beers in hand. He didn't see anyone he knew. He stood in the shadows and watched a young boy light a roman candle.

Bernadette disappeared as she often did at parties. Dwayne stood under a clear desert sky, looking up he saw Jupiter directly overhead. He turned to the southern sky to see if he could identify Betelgeux in Orion's Belt but the horizon was obscured by canyon walls.

He followed the sound of Howlin' Wolf's blues into the house. A few people were milling about in the kitchen where a feast was laid out: beans, enchilada casserole, red and green chili, tortillas, a fruit tray, a chocolate cake with cherries and a bottle of tequila sat on the table. I wish I was hungry, he thought as he sat on a couch beneath a colorful expressionistic painting of an Indian's face; reds and blues and golds and greens. The painting looked like an R.C. Gorman, but it wasn't, just another imitation.

Across the room he recognized Tom Verlaine talking to a woman weighted down with turquoise jewelry. He waved. Verlaine looked at him, but didn't respond. Dwayne yelled across the room. "Verlaine is that you, brother?" A big smile creased Verlaine's face as he squinted in Dwayne's direction. "Dwayne," he said. "How in the heck are you? I didn't recognize you because I'm not wearing my glasses and I'm pretty messed up."

"Yeh, so am I. I ate a couple shrooms before I came to the party."

"You old hippies never die," Verlaine said, eating mushrooms, playing pool, drinking Japanese beer, smoking marijuana. Does your mother know you're acting like this? What are you going to do next?"

Dwayne met Verlaine, a Sioux painter at a recent art opening in Santa Fe. They went out a shot a couple games of pool, talked art and women. Dwayne like the guy and was sorry they hadn't exchange phone numbers.

They laughed and sat on the couch next to Verlaine's girlfriend, an Anglo woman from Chicago, wearing turquoise ear-rings, silver bracelets and cowboy boots.

Dwayne's mind flashed to the night he and Verlaine played pool in Tiny's Lounge. He stroked the 8 ball into a corner pocket and scratched. "Fuck," Dwayne said, loud enough for everyone in the bar to hear it. Two guys at the next table turned their bad eye on him. "What are you guys fuckin' guys looking at?" he said. To himself he said this. I'm too old to fight, he thought. Pretty soon I'll be too old to make love. Then I'll probably get Alzheimer's like my Dad and I won't remember fighting or fucking. That's why my mantra is: "Fuck it. Fuck it. Fuck it."

Verlaine leaned over and whispered in Dwayne's ear, "I love white women, Dwayne. I tell them what they want to hear from a noble savage and they eat it up. I'm a living myth, bro. It's good to see you. I hope you can come to my reading tomorrow night."

"Where is it?"

"At the Aztec Café in Santa Fe. Hey man, let me introduce you to Gail."

"Dwayne's a video artist," Verlaine said, "Gail's a painter."

She told Dwayne she worked in oils and made $25,000 from selling her art last year. Then out of the blue she said, "I work out with weights, too. Do you?"

"Yes, I do," he said, noticing her muscled biceps, he sucked in his stomach.

"What club do you belong to?"

"Club? I don't belong to any clubs. I thought you were a surrealist. Can't you sense you're talking to Dada? Where's your artistic intuition?"

Gail hugged Verlaine's arm a little tighter. Dwayne sensed Gail was accustomed to polite conversations. Poor thing, here she is being confronted by a stoned Dada poet.

"What have I done to deserve this," she thought. "I just want to make love to this Indian, go home to New York and describe my far out west primitive experience to my friends from Sarah Lawrence."

Dwayne got up from the couch and walked into the adjacent room where people were dancing. Teresa Gilberto appeared beside him. He met her at a softball game in Los Alamos just outside the 12 foot high barbed wire fence where the Los Alamos National Laboratory housed 2.7 tons of plutonium.

"You cut your hair," she said.

"Well, thank you for noticing," he said, flipping a limp wrist. "I'm trying on a homosexual persona. What do you think? Does it work for me?"

She stepped in closer. He could smell her horniness.

"Brother, you are so homophobic. Whatever you are, you are not gay. You look sexier than ever. Maybe we'll connect later. I'm staying at the Casino of Gold Motel," she said.

Bernadette was wandering around the party somewhere. He could visualize her coming in the room about now with Teresa rubbing her snatch on his leg. "I'm innocent Bernadette. I didn't do a thing to make her come on to me. In fact, I told her I was gay."

Bernadette didn't walk into the room. Teresa walked away when she saw someone rolling a joint on the kitchen table.

Verlaine was telling Gail about the time he was in a Denver bar on Larimer Street, drinking beer. "A guy sat on the stool next to me," he said. "I turned to acknowledge his presence and he said, 'What are you looking at?' I bought him a beer. Turns out he was Crow. When I told him I was Sioux he called me a dog eater. I told him I didn't appreciate being called a dog eater and wham, he pulled a knife and stabbed me right here in the hand." He held his left hand out for Gail to see and they saw a half moon scar on the back of his hand.

Susan Avery, a potter from Santa Clara Pueblo listened to Verlaine's story from across the room.

"I just pulled the knife out of my hand and licked the blood of the Crow's knife. It hurt like hell, but I've done the Sun Dance and I've learned not to show pain, but…"

"You Sioux guys are tough, huh?" Susan said, pimping him, interrupting his story.

Verlaine acted like he didn't hear her and continued his story. "I grabbed him by the throat and said, 'I think you owe me a drink. If you don't think so I'm going to rip your throat out and bite your nose off. It's your choice. The Crow guy bought me a beer and I kept his knife."

"Now don't get me wrong," Susan said. "But do you Sioux guys really eat dog because I have a friend from North Dakota who told me puppies taste like human flesh." Susan was drunk and in dangerous territory.

"How does your friend know what human flesh tastes like," Verlaine said, breaking the tension. There were about three seconds of silence. Susan took a drink of beer. "I'm just playing with you, man. Tell me were you at Pine Ridge?"

"That was a long time ago and I don't want to talk about it." The mood changed and Susan and Verlaine got into a conversation about skinning rattlesnakes. Susan said they tasted like chicken.

Bernadette tapped Dwayne on the shoulder. "Tara just called," she said. "She wants us to come home so we can light fireworks. Are you ready to go?"

"Hey Verlaine, I've got to go. But let's get together. Are you staying in Santa Fe?"

"It's early, bro. Where you going?"

"I have to go home. My daughter wants us to come home and light fireworks."

They exchanged phone numbers and promised to get together soon. Dwayne and Bernadette walked out into the night blossoming with fireworks.

He stumbled into a cholla cactus and howled like a hyena in labor. "Give me the keys," Bernadette said. "You're too drunk to drive."

When they got home Tara, their nine year old daughter, had roman candles, sparklers and assorted Black Cat's lined up on a picnic table. They shot a couple of bottle rockets, lit a few packs of firecrackers, some sparklers and an M-80. Dwayne got excited about lighting the M-80 because he and his brothers use to sell them on the Black Market. An M-80 is one-eighth of a stick of dynamite. Dwayne lit the M-80 and it went off like a lady finger.

"Really loud Dad," Tara said, laughing and spinning in circles, holding a sparkler above her head.

When all the fireworks were gone they went inside. Tara gave them a kiss and went to be bed. Dwayne and Bernadette drank another beer. Drunk, he looked at Bernadette's classic Hispanic-Jewish profile, feeling like he could taste her beauty.

"I going to bed," she said. "Are you coming?"

"In just a minute. Can I wake you if you're sleeping?"

"Please do," she said, sliding into his arms, kissing him.

He went outside and looked up to the Pojoaque Valley sky, Jupiter directly overhead. Fireworks illuminated the night in fractal patterns of delight. Dogs barked. He went inside, locked the door and went to bed. Bernadette was sleeping. He tried to wake her, but she was too far gone.

"I love you," he whispered in her ear. He curled up beside her and fell asleep.

COYOTE WOMAN

A starless winter sky above Pojoaque Valley, it felt like snow. I walked into Jake's Dirty Shorts Laundromat around 8 p.m. Two people washing clothes; a woman with her six-year old daughter telling her: "Don't try to blackmail me with Santa Claus mommy," and a tall guy with long black hair, dropping quarters into a dryer.

I loaded a washer and sat down to read a magazine. The big guy came over and sat beside me.

"How are you doing?"

"Good. How are you?"

"My name's Lucy Snow Flower."

"Dwayne Evans."

Lucy Flower? I was shocked. Lucy had bulging biceps, stood about 6'2", weighing in at about 195. She wore a New York Yankees baseball cap, a sleeveless black t-shirt with San Diego State in gold lettering and tattered blue jeans.

For a moment I wondered why she sat next to me and aggressively introduced herself. That moment didn't last long.

"Tomorrow night," Lucy said, "I'm going to commit suicide on stage at the Lensic Theatre. I'd like you to shoot the video and believe me it will go viral. I want you to memorialize me forever. But first you need to design a web-site: suicide.com."

"Wait a minute. How do you know I make videos?"

"I watch you on YouTube," she said. "I liked your last one, *Coyote Woman Sings the Blues*. I've created a design for the site. I've even written the advertising text for you.

"Basically here's the deal, suicide.com will give anyone $1000 for the video of their suicide. One-thousand dollars may not sound like much, but if you're committing suicide you're a loser, so forget about it. If you're interested in learning more about our offer please go to suicide.com and we'll have a counselor guide you through the process.

"After you get the suicide videos put them on your site and charge $5.00 to log on. You'll become a millionaire within three months and then you can sell the movie rights to Hollywood."

"And I go to jail and someone makes a movie about suicide. com and I'll make movies from behind bars and become famous and I'm still be in jail. Sorry Lucy, I can't help you out. I'm busy tomorrow night."

"It's your choice. I'm committing suicide whether you video it or not. I just thought you might like to make some easy money."

Lucy asked me if I'd like to hear about her last performance piece. I didn't have anything better to do so I listened.

"I called the piece "Frozen Blood," she said. "I collected eight pints of my blood, it took me over a year. I froze the blood and carved an ice sculpture of myself. Then I sat my frozen self at a computer with the icy fingers on the keys. The room was refrigerated but the blood slowly melted, leaving nothing but bloody fingerprints on the computer's keyboard."

Lights Up. Bare stage, except for a full length mirror next to a small round table. Black flats enclose the actor in a 12'x12' space.

Lucy dances to the Future of Radio, a Noise piece by Khlebnikov. The music is mechanical, a cacophony of cars, bombs, trains, honking, screaming, guns and machine orgasms sans melody, a hint of rhythm.

"Have you ever heard the noise of a butterfly's wing? The noise of a dying sunflower makes me cry." Lucy chants as she dances. She enters into a trance.

"I am giving birth to the dark waters of time..." She picks up a pistol from the table, aims the gun at her image in the mirror. Freezes for ten seconds then continues to dance, waving the gun like a magic wand.

"I am Kali, Isis, Persephone..." She holds the .45 to her head, her stomach, pauses and aims at her image in the mirror. "I am crow, cloud, demon, saint, virgin, mother, whore. I am trans-sexual and I am tired."

She aims the pistol at her image... Lights down. Five beats of silence. Loud gunshot blast. Future of Radio goes silent. Lights up. Lucy's body splayed on the floor, blood leaks from her head. Lights down. Ten seconds later, lights up. Lucy's body's not there. An empty stage. "Future of Radio" heard at a deafening level.

Dwayne catches it all on video. Driving back home to Pojoaque Valley he thinks about erasing Lucy's suicide video. He doesn't.

SNOW FLOWER'S MAY DAY PERFORMANCE

Good evening, my name's Lucy Snow Flower. Before the next poem I'd like to tell you a story. My senior year at UNM, drunk with my friend Susan Bishop, Susan said let's take your boyfriend's car for a ride. He wasn't my boyfriend anymore, but I still had the keys to his Honda. We went joy riding.

Busted, my ex brought charges. The judge gave me a choice, three years in prison or enlist in the Army. I made the wrong choice. Now, I'm back in school, wounded and enraged. I can't play guitar because I've lost mobility in my left hand from a war wound. For a long time I didn't touch the guitar. I'd been reading tons of poetry to assuage my pain. I love the poetry of Rimbaud, Ferlinghetti, Yeats, Howard Hart, Lew Welch, Ted Berrigan, Rage Against the Machine, Basho and Mayakovski.

I wanted to chant their poems. I took my guitar in my gnarled left hand and plucked a rhythm with my right hand, strumming just the low E and high E simultaneously. My left hand did nothing but hold the guitar neck. The simple rhythm I attribute to Phillip Glass' String Quartet for Mishima. The more I goofed around with my guitar poetry chant reciting Master poets' poems, the more this rap *Time of Assassins* came to be. I'd like to perform it for you:

Walking Albuquerque's city streets like a mad dog in heat looking for an angel in a cup of black coffee. I walk in the Frontier Restaurant like I've done ten thousand times before see my friends sitting round talking poetry, eating cinnamon rolls. I join them in a booth beneath a picture of John Wayne. My friend Maria chants Rimbaud and Ferlinghetti, "It's the time of assassins and dangerous madmen. Who among you still speaks of revolution? Sons and daughters of Whitman, sons and daughters of Poe, Lorca and Rimbaud."

After two cups of coffee and a cinnamon roll I jump up to leave and Maria says, "Wait up, Snow. Let's burn one" We disappear into the alley behind the Living Batch and light one up. After a couple hits we start to chant Rage Against the Machine lyrics: "The same people who are bosses are the same people who burn crosses. The same people who are bosses are the same people who burn crosses." Someone yells, "Shut up, I'm trying to sleep." We dial it down.

"You two keep it up, I love it," it's an old woman's voice coming from behind a dumpster. She's lies on a piece of cardboard covered by a plastic sheet. "Keep it up," she says, "you sound like a choir on fire." Maria thanks her and hands her a five dollar bill. "I've got to get going," Maria says. We hug and head off in opposite directions.

I'm walking Albuquerque city streets like a mad dog in heat, looking for an angel in a cup of black coffee. The last time I saw Jesus was in a North Valley mission, drinking red kool aid from a white plastic cup. I didn't hear any angels, didn't have any visions, just saw down and out men and women drinking red kool aid from white plastic cups. Sirens wail and people scream, gunshots, the city's on fire. I can't seem to forget this dream. Revolution is in the air. Quiet as apricot snow. Quiet as a trigger finger.

MARMALADE COCKROACH

-Performed by Lucy Snow Flower. She's wears a cockroach mask, a black t-shirt, black jeans and is barefoot.

I'm a blue-collar worker, working for Manpower shredding secret documents up in Bomb City at the Los Alamos National Laboratory, home of the Atomic bomb.

Yeh, I'm radioactive. So what? I'm not afraid to glow. The mystics are always talking about "the light...the light." And that's what I'm talking about. I glow and tick, too. Just set me down next to a Geiger counter and I'll make the mother-fucker come.

My name is Marmalade. Marmalade Cockroach. I created myself as an experiment. When I'm hungry, I eat my legs, which are made of marmalade. The flavors change to suit my taste.

When a Voodoo Shaman slices the neck of a rooster, you can hear silence where blood kisses stone. Here at the black tunnel of silence we cease to exist. Are you ready for another war, simulated terror, another ton of oil based body bags, concentration camps?

"No money in peace, boys. Let's start something in Iraq, then Afghanistan. It'll be good for business, besides those damned Muslim pagan babies need some Jesus Christ converting. Don't you agree, Mike?"

"I sure do, Mr. President. The only thing that bothers me is how are we going to have a war without whores? You know how twisted the Muslims are, they don't even have whore houses."

"Well Mike, we'll just have to hire us some putas and import them into the middle-east."

"You're right, Mr. President. You're right again."

"If we play it right, we won't have to nuke New York City. Not yet anyway."

Vice-president Pence kisses President Trump with a wet open mouthed French kiss, getting lipstick on the President's collar.

"Now look what you've done. I told you to be careful. You don't want our wives finding out about us do you?"

Here at the Black Tunnel of Silence we cease to exist. "Time," the Mayan Kid says, "is a long illusionary train. To your left the caboose. To your right, the engine. You can go either way, Senora Marmalade, your looking back is looking back at you. When you touch rock, tree, child, you are rock, tree, child, sleeping in a crystal bed, your masks on fire. The shadow of Mr. Burroughs hangs in the closet. In the window, Einstein's last breath."

Forever, as in dreams, you think you're alone until you notice you have your dog's eyes and your father's hands are your hands. Your veins are the roots of rain. And a falling star is your dead grandmother, calling her children home."

Were we blind and deaf, we would touch hands and talk. Witness a kind of never been there in your footprints. Brothers and Sisters, will you marry the light, or the Atomic City nightmare?

It is, is not, a repeating universe. Beauty's garden tends a burning universe. Moonlit tears, inside each tear the face of an Aztec Butterfly. It is, is not, a repeating universe.

Gnarly, twisted, wrinkled and wet, a homeless man on a L.A. street corner waits for the light to change. He turns to me, says, "I spent five years in Nazi Germany. Hitler's fascist regime reminds me of America 2020."

Nazis in the Whitehouse. Who said that? What? When? Who among you still talks of revolution? Sons of Whitman, sons of Poe, sons of Lorca and Rimbaud. Thomas Jefferson said, "Revolution every seven years."

So what? So what?

Déjà vu, another was fought for drugs and oil and the CIA is the world's largest distributor of cocaine and heroin, therefore, a War on Drugs is a War on the CIA and a War on the CIA is a War on the Whitehouse. So, finally the ultimate absurdity. Read the headlines:

THE UNITED STATES DECLARES WAR ON ITSELF.

Ah yes, the government of the United States is keeping Mr. and Mrs. Banality free. Free to watch whatever TV channel they choose. What a country. Walmart, Kansas is everywhere, just like God used to be.

Haven't heard many good jokes about the Drug War have you? You know why? Because it's not very funny. A citizen can't even find a bag of weed for less than $40. It's turning me into an alcoholic.

Who cares? Who cares? Who cares?

On every street corner, in every North American village, Lady Macbeth stands in blinking neon pools, washes her hands, but the blood remains. Nothing works, not even Ajax.

It is, is not, a repeating universe where Big Mama Moon, the Cosmic Hooker, waits for her pimps: Mr. Shadow, Mr. Terror and Mr. Gravity to pull their red Cadillac up to her body's cool quivering flame, illuminating this massive oil slick around our body, the Tribal Mind.

JAIL BREAK

Dear Snow,

I want to free the children. I know it sounds crazy but I need your help to free my friend's 8 year old niece from the migrant detention center in Clint, Texas just outside of El Paso. We can do it. After the shit we did in Afghanistan we can stage a jail break, open the cages and open minds. I've already talked to Dwayne and he's in. What else do you have to do? We'll need to communicate by phone; you know the throw away ones you can buy at Wal-Mart, definitely no communications on the internet.

Can't wait to see you,

Dante

Lucy read Dante's letter and thought, "Crazy mother-fucker. Now I have to go buy a damn phone, just what I want to do, buy a phone."

Dante's phone rings. He's in the cobra position, descends to the yoga mat, breathing out, stands and answers the telephone.

"Hello,"

"I'd like to start our conversation with a joke. If we're going to talk jail break, I think we should begin with a joke.

Why did Karl Marx hate classical music?" "I'll bite," Dante said. "Why did Karl Marx hate classical music" "Because of the violins inherent in the system."

"Funny. Do you want to get serious, or tell jokes?"

"Well, you could at least have said, 'Lucy, how you doing.' Dante, I would like to get serious and joke around because you're a fool if you think you can break into a federal facility, stage a jail break and get away with it."

"Will you just connect with your heart and listen?"

"I'm listening. Wait a second while I try off the TV."

"I'm working as a guard at the detention center for a private contractor. The security here is amateur league. I have two guards, both vets, in for the project. You're going to drive a Tyson Meat truck into the facility."

"What am I doing driving a truck? I'm a trained killer. Come on man, can't you change the script and give me a speaking part?"

"You've always had a hard time listening. Give me a break, Lucy. Just listen."

"I'm listening."

"The truck driver eats supper at the same café every Friday evening. Your job is to hijack the truck. It will be dark when he leaves the café. You'll knock him out with a stun gun, handcuff him and throw him in the truck. You then drive to the facility where the guard will let you in because he's with us. Meanwhile, we're torching a building to create havoc. With security turned to the fire, we'll slip ten kids out onto the loading ramp where they board the truck. You drive away to a pick-up point where you'll ditch the truck for an SUV, from there you drive to a safe house in Mexico and walk away."

"Sorry, Dante I'm busy this week."

"Did I mention $100,000? Some of these kids have connections with rich Mexicans."

"What are you talking about? You are fucking delusional."

"And you aren't listening. The rich Mexicans are connected to the drug trade."

"You're talking the Sinaloa cartel?"

"Right."

"Why doesn't the cartel stage the jail break?"

"For over a decade, under multiple administrations, the U.S. government has had a secret agreement with the Sinaloa cartel that allowed it to operate with impunity. The cartel made a deal with the government not to get involved in internal USA political affairs. If the CIA thinks they staged the jail break all hell would break lose for the cartel. They are businessmen and they want to contract the job to an outside source."

"I want $200,000 and I want paid up front."

"I think they'll agree to that."

"If they do, I'm in. With $200,000 I can become a ghost and disappear."

PERFORMANCE ART

I opened my laptop, clicked on Google images and typed in red because I wanted a mono-chromatic screen saver, scrolling down the page I saw a picture of a group of people with white mime faces, dressed in red. I clicked on the image and read about a performance group in England called The Red Brigade. The Red Brigade is a political performance group, their goal to heighten awareness about the eminent danger of global warming. I felt my spirit lift as I read because I've been in despair about the global cannibalism that has experts predicting the ringing of civilization's death knell.

Having survived the horrors of war, I am haunted by nightmares because the apocalypse is upon us. What to do? My thoughts ran from political assassination, to self-immolation chained to the White House fence, staging a jail break at one of the child detention centers, to suicide, to terrorism, to massive non-violent demonstrations. The Red Brigade's performance art was a call to action.

Investigating the Red Brigade on YouTube I found they are aligned with Extinction Rebellion, an anarchist movement whose philosophy is radical non-violence. They are aggressive in their non-violence, blocking city streets and threatening to fly drones over Heathrow to stop air traffic. They are often arrested. I've been in jail and I didn't enjoy the time spent.

I recently read a story about a guy's first day in prison. He watched two men brawl in the bloodiest, most animalistic fight he'd ever seen. He asked an inmate why they were fighting. "There fighting to see who fucks you first."

No, I don't need to be inside but I do need to do something even if it is pissing in the wind. The apocalypse is at hand and the end is near if we don't transform to an international socialism that attempts to bring an end to global warming. Suddenly, as I'm writing this, a voice in my head says "bullshit." My t-shirt has Toast scrawled across the front, because I recently heard Noam Chomsky say, "If Trump is re-elected president, we're toast."

Snow called me last night and told me about her plans to go to El Paso to help Dante free some kids from a detention center.

"Snow, there's no way you'll get away with this. The feds will be all over this case. You will be caught."

"Maybe not, besides it's doing something real, something patriotic. It'll raise awareness about the monstrous conditions inside the prison."

"It will make things worse. They'll bring in more security. The whole prison atmosphere will become more draconian, the children will still suffer and your idealism will end you up in Leavenworth."

"What are you going to do, hot shot? Drink coffee, smoke dope and write a book that no one will ever read."

"Exactly. That's what I'm going to do. And I'm going to get back together with Francesca. I'm turning my life around. We're creating a performance art group called The Holy Ghost Brigade. We're going to do what we have to do to engender transformation."

"Does that mean you're ready to kill someone that you judge to be evil? I thought you were a pacifist."

"I can't say I'm that desperate but I do believe righteous indignation can lead to an art form called murder. Today sitting in my car outside Sprout's Market I noticed about 20% of the people entering the supermarket were not wearing masks. I felt violent, enraged. From a purely selfish point of few I don't want coronavirus in my face. Would I actually kill someone, probably not, but it's a possibility. Why don't you join us?"

"No way, T.J. I've got a major role to play in Dante's Jail Break. After this show I'm taking a long vacation."

"Good luck, sister. Tell Dante if he's lucky he'll receive death as a reward. And if you survive, I'm sure you'll get time off for good behavior."

THE HOLY GHOST BRIGADE

Our costumes were an essential part of our act. We wore flowing blue velvet floor length gowns with a knotted blue headdress that looked Bedouin. Our faces painted mime white. Our lips painted red.

Our first performance was in Los Alamos, birthplace of the atomic bombs that fell on Hiroshima and Nagasaki, killing over 200,000 people. We parked the car on the street and slowly walked towards Ashley Pond at the center of town, holding erect mime postures. We tried to flow as much as possible. Beside the lake, we stood facing each other six feet apart. For ten minutes we were blue statues, our arms reaching out in a desperate attempt to touch. About a dozen people gathered around us.

"What are they doing?" someone said, just what I wanted to hear. We were open to interpretation. We were silent stone statues. At the end of the tableau we mimed walked to the street, hopped in our car and drove away. That night, Francesca and I made love for the first time, again.

John Knoll was born in Neosho, Missouri. He received a B.S. in Social Work from Pittsburg State College in Pittsburg, Kansas. He and Joe Speer edited *Tortilla* and *Chameleon Magazines*. His books include *Magic Vessel, Wrestling the Wheel, Ghosting America, Elevator Music for the Dead, Opera of Virus, Hummingbird Graffiti* and a spoken word cd *Black Wing* with John Macker. He has performed his poetry with rock and jazz bands, most notably the Jack Kerouac Band and Nuclear Trout. He currently makes his living as a free-lance journalist from his home in Pojoaque, New Mexico.

This project was made possible, in part, by generous support from the Osage Arts Community.

Osage Arts Community provides temporary time, space and support for the creation of new artistic works in a retreat format, serving creative people of all kinds — visual artists, composers, poets, fiction and nonfiction writers. Located on a 152-acre farm in an isolated rural mountainside setting in Central Missouri and bordered by ¾ of a mile of the Gasconade River, OAC provides residencies to those working alone, as well as welcoming collaborative teams, offering living space and workspace in a country environment to emerging and mid-career artists. For more information, visit us at www.osageac.org

CPSIA information can be obtained
at www.ICGtesting.com
Printed in the USA
BVHW071632181220
595733BV00002B/214